The Pen Pieyu Adventures

Sir Princess Petra

BOOKS BY DIANE MAE ROBINSON

Sir Princess Petra
The Pen Pieyu Adventures

Sir Princess Petra's Talent
The Pen Pieyu Adventures

Sir Princess Petra's Mission
The Pen Pieyu Adventures

The Dragon Grammar Book
Grammar for Kids, Dragons,
and the Whole Kingdom

The Forest Painter

The Pen Pieyu Adventures

Sir Princess Petra

Book 1

Diane Mae Robinson

Sir Princess Petra – The Pen Pieyu Adventures
Copyright © 2011 by Diane Mae Robinson. All rights reserved.

First published in 2011 by Tate Publishing & Enterprises, LLC
Second edition published by Diane Mae Robinson Ink, September,
2017

This novel is a work of fiction. Names, descriptions, entities, and
incidents included in the story are products of the author's
imagination. Any resemblance to actual persons, events, and entities is
entirely coincidental.

Illustrations by Samantha Kickingbird

Published in Canada

ISBN: 978-1-988714-05-9
·1. Juvenile Fiction / Readers / Chapter Books
·2. Juvenile Fiction / Action & Adventure / General

Dedication

For Dezi, Kiyah, and Izzak

Praise for *Sir Princess Petra: The Pen Pieyu Adventures, Book 1*

Her writing grabs you, is perfectly pitched, nuanced, a fresh approach.

—Lieutenant Governor of Alberta
Emerging Artist Award adjudicators

The Pen Pieyu Adventures: Sir Princess Petra is a maverick fantasy, packed with plot twists and turns, unexpected obstacles and problems, and brilliant flashes of humor and originality. *Sir Princess Petra* charms and entrances the reader.

—Midwest Book Review

Sir Princess Petra is an empowering, delightfully imaginative story. Petra's character is both confident and charismatic. I highly recommend *Sir Princess Petra* for school, public, and personal library collections.

—University of Manitoba Reviews

This is a great book for elementary schools and public libraries. I would highly recommend this book.

—Brenda Ballard for Readers' Favorite

Praise for *Sir Princess Petra's Talent: The Pen Pieyu Adventures, Book 2*

I love this book series! *Sir Princess Petra's Talent* is a wonderful, fast-paced story full of humor and profound messages—what a powerful combination!
—Alinka Rutkowska, award winning children's author

Diane Mae Robinson's second book in *The Pen Pieyu Adventures* series is a delightful read and one that is sure to engage and enthrall young readers.
    —Children's Literary Classics Int'l Book Awards

A fairy tale enriched with magical worlds. The book that we want to define as a graceful masterpiece in children's literature.
                                        —Advices Books

Diane Mae Robinson's fantasy adventure tale, *Sir Princess Petra's Talent*, is quite simply wonderful.
                        —Jack Magnus for Readers' Favorite

Praise for *Sir Princess Petra's Mission: The Pen Pieyu Adventures, Book 3*

The degree of imagination is matched by the terrific humor and sense of fun. From the beginning chapter to the end, this book is a treasure and one that is highly recommended.
—Grady Harp, Top 100 Amazon Reviewer

The third title in author Diane Mae Robinson's outstanding *The Pen Pieyu Adventures* series is an impressive and thoroughly entertaining read and very highly recommended.
—Midwest Book Review

An enchanting book, filled with wry humor and titillating prose, sort of Dr. Seuss without the rhyme.
—Charles A. Ray, author

More reviews for *The Pen Pieyu Adventures* series:
https://www.dragonsbook.com

Awards for *Sir Princess Petra: The Pen Pieyu Adventures, Book 1*

2012 Lieutenant Governor of Alberta Emerging Artist Award (literary arts)
2012 Purple Dragonfly Book Award
2013 Readers' Favorite International Book Award
2014 Sharp Writ Book Award

Awards for *Sir Princess Petra's Talent: The Pen Pieyu Adventures, Book 2*

2014 Readers' Favorite International Book Award
2015 Children's Literary Classics Seal of Approval
2015 Children's Literary Classics Book Award
2015 Los Angeles Book Festival Book Award
2015 Purple Dragonfly Book Award

Awards for *Sir Princess Petra's Mission: The Pen Pieyu Adventures, Book 3*

2016 Readers' Favorite International Book Award
2016 Book Excellence Award

TABLE OF CONTENTS

MAP OF
PEN PIEYU KINGDOM
AND SURROUNDING LANDS

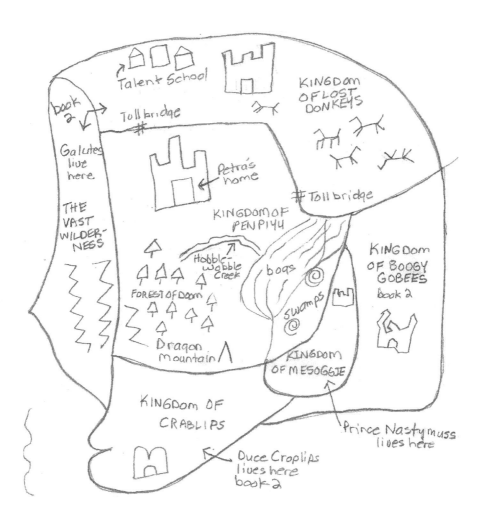

Talent School

KINGDOM OF LOST DONKEYS

book 2

Toll bridge

Galutes live here.

THE VAST WILDERNESS

Petra's home

Toll bridge

KINGDOM OF PENPIYU

Hobble-Wobble Creek

bogs

KINGDOM OF BOOGY GOBEES book 2

FOREST OF Doom

swamps

Dragon mountain

KINGDOM OF MESOGGJE

KINGDOM OF CRABLIPS

Prince Nastymuss lives here

Duce Crablips lives here book 2

Diane Mae Robinson

CHAPTER 1

THE PRINCESS

Petra curtsied to the king and queen of Pen Pieyu, who sat upon their ragged, leather thrones.

"Father, tomorrow is the ninth day of the ninth month of the ninth year."

"Yes, my dear princess, it is your royal birthday. And according to royal custom, you may have anything your heart desires, as promised," declared King Longstride.

"I have thought hard and for many passing moons. Jewels, frocks of lace, and princess games have become boring. The thing I want the most . . ." Petra hesitated and bit on her lip. "I want to be a royal knight."

"A knight!" The king bolted upright and made his eyes grow buggy huge. The queen swiped her hand over her forehead and moaned. The royal councilman got so excited he ran around in circles until he was dizzy, which then caused him to bump into a royal pillar and splatter onto the floor.

"Why, never have I heard such a strange request," the king said while pacing and scratching his grey beard. "You are a princess . . . a girl. One must be big and brave and mean and nasty to be a royal knight."

"Where is it written that a girl cannot be a knight and protect her kingdom?" Petra demanded.

The royal councilman immediately fetched the royal rule book. After a flurry of page flipping, he stopped on a page and guided his finger down the lines as he mumble-read from the book. "It does not say anything about such a matter, Your Majesty. There is no rule regarding princesses or girls attaining, or not attaining, knighthood."

The king put on his crescent-moon grin and winked at the woozy-looking queen. He turned the book toward him, flipped a few pages forward, and read: "To become a knight of Kingdom Pen Pieyu, a potential knight must choose an act of bravery from the royal list of deeds. The choices are: to capture a crocodile and make his skin into a royal leather chair; to hush that howling, nasty dragon, Snarls, in the Forest of Doom; or to eat a roomful of raw onions."

Petra peeked into the royal onion room. All nine of the palace soldiers were crying and munching away. "Yuck, I will never eat onions! And the only crocodile I know lives in the moat and is my friend. I have no choice, I will hush the howling dragon, Snarls, in the Forest of Doom," she announced.

Promptly, the queen fainted. The king groaned and shook his head in disbelief, then plopped down onto his ragged, leather royal chair.

"But I will take a sack of onions with me," Petra added.

The royal chef grumbled while he outfitted the princess with a suit of his best royal pots and pans—the regular armour had turned out to be much too large. Lastly, the royal chef handed her a sword, which, Petra thought, seemed to resemble one of the royal cake knives.

Petra clunked out of the palace. "Goodbye, and don't worry. I will throw onions at the beast until he cries and surrenders. If need be, I will stab him in the foot with my sword. See, I can be a nasty, big meany."

CHAPTER 2

THE QUEST

The princess clomped, clattered, and clanked into the Forest of Doom. Shadows seemed to be reaching out to grab her, and she thought she heard the wind whisper a warning.

A tremendous screech vibrated the air just before a hawk as big as the royal mule swooped down, talons spread wide. Petra ducked just as the hawk's claws rattled upon the pot on her head, and in a flash the hawk stole off with her helmet. With all her might, Petra flung an onion at the thieving bird. The shot missed him by a jousting lance length, ricocheted off a tree, then bounced off a hanging nest that sent a swarm of now homeless, angry bees diving after the hawk.

"Ha! See, I am not afraid! I am a big, rude . . . or was it . . . mean and rotten?" She shook her fist toward the sky. "I am a knight! Well, just about." The hawk and trailing bees circled round, plunging straight toward her. She turned and ran.

As she neared Dragon Mountain, deeper in the Forest of Doom, something rustled and grunted in the willows. Two yellow eyes glared out at her. Petra pointed her sword, but it seemed to shake all on its own, so she sliced it back and forth through the air, making it whistle. "Come out, you coward," she ordered. A bristle-haired beast burst through the willows, charging two pointy tusks straight at her. Petra squished one eye shut and squinted with the other.

The beast brushed past her, spinning her around. This sent her sword spinning and flying until the sword landed in the curve of the beast's tusks.

"You reckless boar!" she hollered, but only after the pig had galloped far into the distance. "Come back with my sword."

††††††††††††††

An eerie howl echoed through the misty mountain air. The spruce trees seemed to shiver and shake and shimmy just like Petra's knees. Snarls the dragon was definitely near.

"A brave must be . . . no, a knight means to be . . . no, no, no. A true, brave knight must be mean and nasty—that's it!" she cried out, finally recalling her father's words.

Now, through the branches, she spied Snarls huffing and snorting out puffs of smoke. Huge green eyes under bumpy eyelids glared back at her. Without hesitating, Petra sprang out from behind the trees and hurled onions at the dragon's eyes. The dragon raised his head, heaving out a swirling, fiery blast from his flared nostrils. Petra cringed as the heat of his foul breath surged past her.

"Ow!" The princess rubbed her face and stomped her foot. "You nearly singed my eyebrows off!"

"Well, you threw onions at me," Snarls grumbled back.

Petra grabbed a pointy branch that was on the ground beside her. Levelling her new weapon at the dragon's nose, she stared her meanest stare. "I am here to hush you, you nasty, howling dragon. Then I will become a brave and royal knight."

For a moment, the dragon looked confused. Then his glistening scales jiggled in rhythm with his growing laughter. "Ha ha ha! So, that's why, ha ha ha ha, soldier after soldier barges into my forest. They throw arrows, stones, the odd rock-hard meat pie, and now onions. Then they hightail it out of here when I get mad and blast them. Ha ha ha ha ha!" The dragon clutched his belly like he had a stomach ache.

"Well . . . yes," Petra stammered. She eyed the dragon suspiciously. "Your howling has become quite annoying, you know. No one in the castle has slept in weeks, and everyone is getting quite cranky. Maybe you, Mr. Smarty-Pants Dragon, have a better idea?"

"You, the smallest of soldiers, are the first to ask. And just for the record, most of my so-called howling is my serenading the forest creatures, lulling them to sleep with my magnificent voice and, occasionally, singing requests by the full moon. But lately, I must admit, I have been doing a lot of not-so-magnificent howling. As you see, I have a little predicament here." Snarls flashed a wide, pleading grin as he pointed to his tail that was pinned under a pile of rocks at the mouth of the cave. "And I would certainly stop my not-so-magnificent howling if you could help me out."

Petra let out a little chuckle, untied the leather strings that held her armour, and climbed the rock pile. She tossed stone after stone, pleased with how quickly the pile dwindled, until she spotted the boulder. "Why, it's the size of the royal goat—"

Clunk. Something knocked Petra on the head and clanked to the ground.

"My helmet!" she cheered but soon remembered where she had lost it. She peered up. The hawk and trailing bees looked like a giant arrowhead shooting toward her.

"Hurry, try to pull your tail out!" Petra grunted, forcing all her weight against the boulder. Snarls twisted and wiggled and pulled.

Finally, the boulder let loose and toppled over. Petra

half-leaped, half-tumbled behind the boulder just as dagger-like claws snatched at her ponytail.

Snarls let out a whoop and swished his freed tail back and forth. The whirlwind current created by his swinging tail sent the hawk and bees scattering.

"Thank you." Petra sighed.

"No, thank you, the smallest of soldiers." Snarls took a long bow. "And for your gallant services, I will sincerely try humming to the forest creatures from now on; maybe just the occasional tiny, little howl to the full moon."

Petra giggled. She noticed the dragon shift his admiring gaze away from her, toward the pots and pans.

"Snarls, you should keep these. Anyway, I won't be needing them now that I'll be a royal knight and have my own armour suited."

Snarls clicked his claws together. "They'll be perfect for my next barbeque event. You will come, won't you?"

"Of course. Just give a howl," Petra answered with a wink. "A short one, mind you."

The princess and dragon clutched hand and paw, and they laughed.

CHAPTER 3

THE ROYAL STEED

Early the next day, after a much-needed good night's sleep, Petra entered the royal throne room and bowed to the king and queen. They smiled at her with beaming faces.

"Petra, my dear, you have accomplished a great deed by hushing that howling dragon," the king said, "and tonight we shall throw you a grand knighting party. All the kingdom shall attend to praise and honor you and hear tell of your tale." He turned toward the queen and spoke in a hushed voice, "And, hopefully, bring many, many gifts for the kingdom."

"Yes, Father, that shall be swell." Petra straightened her posture. "I would like to request that Snarls attend as my royal steed."

The king slumped down in his chair, rolled his eyes like he just got whacked on the head, and signaled the royal councilman to approach. The royal councilman whirled around for a full minute, two fingers pressed to his temple, then scurried off toward the royal bathroom to promptly return with the royal rule book.

The queen moaned and muttered as she flopped her head onto the side wing of her chair. "Why can't she just be a normal princess?"

Flipping the pages of the royal rule book, the royal

councilman finally found the page and pointed to a section.

The king mumbled, huffed, and harrumphed as he read. "Well, it appears the rule declares that a royal knight may choose his royal steed from anywhere in the lands of Pen Pieyu Kingdom. The only stipulation is that the steed have four legs." The king re-read the rule to himself. "So vague. Such nonsense."

"You wrote it," the queen reminded him.

The king puffed out his chest. "The oil lamp must have gone out while I was in the middle of forming a thought."

Petra chuckled as she imagined the alternative kinds of steeds.

The king looked up, his eyebrows twitching; his face didn't look so beaming anymore. He raised his arms in surrender. "Request granted."

Petra raced off to the armoury to fetch her new suit of armour. The blacksmith had done a fine job. The breastplate and chain mail leggings were lightweight and easy to put on. She thought the armour a tad too shiny but was impressed by the huge pink plume on top of the helmet, just as she had requested. She collected her new sword, which still looked very much like a cake knife, and her bag of onions before trotting out of the castle.

CHAPTER 4

THE BOG ENCOUNTER

At the edge of the Forest of Doom, Petra peered into its darkness, and a shiver crept up her neck. "I am a royal knight," she announced to the forest, "and therefore, I will go around your shadowy woods to fetch my royal steed."

The bogs and swamps of Pen Pieyu Kingdom, bordering the lands of Mesoggie, were mushy and cumbersome, smelling of foul things. And there were sink holes to watch out for. But the brightness of the day cheered her spirits—until she noticed a strange black blob up ahead. The shadowy figure seemed to be floating toward her with dark intentions. Petra halted so fast that the plume on her helmet swatted her face before flipping back again. Her heart did a flip when she recognized the figure. It was Bograt, the bog witch.

Before Petra could gather her wits, the scruffy-looking bog witch flung out a leather whip that wrapped around Petra's leg and hauled her down.

"Leave me be, Bograt," Petra squealed, trying to free herself from the whip and the muck. "I am a royal knight on a mission, and you are interfering with my mission."

Bograt cackled. "Ha! You, a royal knight? You are a

pip-squeak playing in costume, and I shall have you for dinner."

Petra felt all hot and sticky and couldn't catch her breath. She tried to grasp her sword but her trembling hand let it fall.

Bograt pushed her.

"Don't be such a bully, Bograt. I am a royal knight, as I say. And you should know what the penalty in the royal rule book is for interfering in a knight's mission, or any person in the kingdom on a mission, for that matter. You were told all the bog rules the last time you were hauled into the castle for meddling with Peasant Clever."

"Yuck." Bograt cringed and scrunched up her mud-crusted face. "They'll try to wash me and put me in a frilly dress again. And worse for messing with a knight. Forget it. I believe you. You're free to go."

Bograt, giving a lopsided grin, extended her hand to help Petra up from the slimy mud.

Petra smiled, remembering Bograt squirming and yelping as five royal maids scrubbed her clean, then fitted her into a frilly dress with mountains of itchy lace.

Bograt started sniffing the air as Petra picked up her sword and sack.

"Is that onions I smell?" Bograt asked in a sing-song voice.

Surprised by Bograt's pleasant tone, Petra opened her sack to show the bog witch her stash of onions.

"Oh, goody, goody, goody." Bograt hopped from one foot to the other. "Give them to me."

Petra frowned her eyebrows.

"Okay, there's a word for that . . . um . . . peas. No, that's not it. Hmmm." Bograt scratched her ear until a pebble fell out. "How about plea. No?" The bog witch grimaced. "Okay, have it your way. Please is the word. Please it shall be. Please give me some onions to make onion soup."

An idea came to Petra. "You may have some onions now and many more later—on one condition. You stop frightening people and animals, and quit threatening to eat them; that includes frogs, which you probably savor in your witchy potions.

Bograt showed a wide smile of blue-stained teeth. "Well, I don't really eat people, animals, or slimy frogs. Probably a nasty taste. I agree, then."

Petra handed her two onions.

Bograt scurried off like a maniac. "Remember our onion deal then, missy knight," she hollered over her shoulder to Petra.

"I will! Whenever you need more onions, come by the castle and I'll give you a whole sack full."

In a clearing, just at the edge of the Forest of Doom, Petra found Snarls curled up and napping. The pots and pans she had left for him were washed and drying in the sun. She tip-toed closer and tapped his nose. Snarls snored out a small fire stream before opening one eye.

"Yeow!" Petra shrieked, slapping sparks off her plume.

"Oh, little knight, it's you. Sorry about that." Snarls yawned and stretched and puffed out a few curls of smoke. "You can't be too careful around sleeping dragons, you know. Nice suit, by the way."

"I'm all right, Snarls. And thanks. About the suit, I mean." Petra brushed the remaining ashes off her face. "I have great news. I've chosen you to be my royal steed and my guest for my knighting party tonight."

Snarls tilted his head and narrowed his left eye. "The king approved this?" he questioned.

Petra nodded.

"Will there be food? Maybe a barbeque? Should I whip up a dish of one of my specialities?" Snarls clicked his claws together with rapid rhythm.

"You don't need to bring anything—the royal chefs will prepare the feast. Will you come to the party? Will you agree to be my royal steed?"

"Mount up, my brave, little knight. We're going to shake some claws and feet and have ourselves a humdinger of a party."

CHAPTER 5

PRINCE NASTYBUN

Petra laughed and Snarls snorted as they told jokes about the want-to-be knights on their mission to eat a roomful of raw onions back at the castle. As they trotted through the Forest of Doom, Petra felt a warm, fuzzy feeling come over her, and she noticed that the shadows didn't seem as menacing as before. Just as Snarls finished a particularly bad joke about how the want-to-be knights could fight an army by blowing them over with their onion breath, a small and peculiar knight mounted on a Welsh pony appeared out of nowhere.

Snarls reined in with a big *whoa* just short of bowling him over.

Petra stared, rubbed her eyes, and stared again at the strange-looking knight.

The knight in dented, moss-covered black armour pointed his sword toward Petra and spoke in a high-pitched voice that sounded like a screeching violin. "I am Prince Norton Nastybun from Kingdom Mesoggie. And these are my devious, fearless, and devoted knights." He gestured toward a bunch of puny knights on puny ponies hiding amongst the trees.

"This is quite the strange situation," Petra whispered to Snarls.

"And stranger as they're all midgets," Snarls whispered back.

Everybody just blinked and stared at each other for some time until Petra asked, "Is there something we can do for you?"

"We're here for the duel, of course," Prince Nastybun scoffed.

"What's a do-well?" Snarls asked.

"It's a duel, not a do-well," Petra answered. "They want to fight."

"Fight?" Snarls growled and let loose a swirl of smoke.

Norton Nastybun removed his purple, knitted gloves and looked to be in a huff. "Are you not the princess royal knight?" he asked, sounding annoyed.

"Yes," Petra replied. "But what does that have to do with a duel?"

"My father, King Nastybun of Kingdom Mesoggie, sent a scroll to your father, King Longstride of Kingdom Pen Pieyu, many new moons ago, stating that if Kingdom Pen Pieyu ever acquired royal knights—" the puny army broke into laughter at this last part "—that we would challenge his kingdom in a duel for possession of Pen Pieyu lands."

"But I am the only royal knight," Petra said, wondering at her father's forgetfulness on such an important matter.

"All the easier for us." Nastybun signaled his army of puny knights. In unison, the puny knights raised their swords and marched their puny ponies forward.

Petra felt a wiggly feeling in her stomach, and it didn't feel good.

"What is your answer?" Prince Nastybun prodded.

"I'm trying to think." Petra couldn't remember learning anything about how a royal knight should fight since Pen Pieyu Kingdom never had a royal knight before her. She was sure it was nasty business, though.

Snarls growled and lowered his head until he was eyeball to eyeball with Norton. "I could just blast them all to puny smithereens."

"No, Snarls. That would be un-knightly, just as nine knights against one knight is un-knightly." Sweat was forming under her helmet, and her head was buzzing and felt light, like it might float away. Her dizzy feeling straightened out though, when she thought of her mother's silly fainting spells.

"Just you and me then," Prince Nastybun said, sounding very sure of himself. The puny prince titled in his saddle, spilled awkwardly off his pony, and landed with an unruly thump on the ground. With flushed cheeks, he instantly sprang upright.

Petra patted Snarls' neck. Snarls lower himself, and she slid down the polished scales of her mount.

The pair met in the middle. Prince Nastybun put up his fists and swirled them around all the while attempting some fancy foot maneuvers that looked more like he had ants in his pants than it did any fighting tactic. The faster he hopped around, the louder the odd, squishy sound coming from his boots became. His band of puny knights broke into cheers and whistles.

Snarls cheered and hooted and hollered louder. "Charge on, Petra, you brave and royal knight. Give that pint-size prince a badge of black and blue to take home."

Petra stood up tall, took a deep breath, and went straight into her highland dance routine. Arms poised and feet flashing, Petra was sure she would somehow dazzle the prince into—

Norton Nastybun clobbered her with a punch to the nose.

"That is just plain mean!" Petra wiggled her nose and

couldn't help the rapid blinking of her eyes.

"Do you give up?"

"No, I do not give up!"

"Are you going to cry?" Nastybun asked. He grinned a sly grin. The puny knights fell to the ground, laughing and rolling over each other in their fit of hysterics.

"No, but watch this." Petra started up her dance again, tapping, kicking, and twirling, faster and faster. The prince slowly lowered his sword, cocked his head, then sprouted a cockeyed look on his face. Soon Petra was close enough to grab him around the chest and clutch him in a bear hug. There was a peculiar, musty odor about him, but she hung on tight nonetheless. With his arms pinned to his sides, there was nothing the prince could do but let her dance and squeeze and twirl and squeeze and dance . . . .

One by one, the puny knights, then finally Snarls, grew bored of watching the endless dance and decided to make a fire and roast some mushrooms.

Prince Nastybun was looking somewhat stunned or maybe just fully dizzy when Petra asked him, "Are you ready to give up yet? Because I will dance and hug you until you have no choice but to hug me back and stop this ridiculous nonsense."

Norton broke into tears and said he would hug her back, which he did, as soon as she let go of him. "It's really not my fault," he sobbed. "Father put me up to this. He tries to be mean and nasty because our kingdom is so puny and wet. We're always wet living in those soggy lands. I'm really not mean and nasty at all."

Petra took off his helmet to stroke his head and console him. She was amazed when long, black ringlets sprang out. "It will all right," she assured him. "But I must say, your kingdom certainly has made itself a nasty reputation around here. Believe me, you don't have to be mean and nasty to get things done. We'll talk to my father. I'm sure he will allow you and your kingdom's people to come to our lands whenever you want. That way, you can all dry out sometimes."

"That would be nice." Prince Nastybun sniffled.

"Hey, Petra! You got some onions over there?" Snarls called out. "She always carries onions." He shrugged his shoulders as he explained to the puny army.

Petra and Norton made their way over to the rest of the group. They all feasted on mushrooms and onions that Snarls roasted to perfection. Except Petra, who had her roasted mushrooms plain.

CHAPTER 6

GOING HOME

The fading sunlight allowed the forest shadows to thrive and the mosquitoes' buzzing to swell into a chaotic hum. Petra proposed that they all head back to the castle for the night and to attend her knighting party.

"We should cross at Hobble-Wobble Creek," Petra suggested after noticing Snarls and the whole puny army moaning and rubbing their bellies—from eating nearly all her onions, she guessed. "It will be quicker than trudging through the tricky bogs at night."

Snarls let out a tremendous burb and moaned louder. "They don't call it Hobble-Wobble Creek for nothing, you know. I hear tell that sheep have lost their ears, cows come home with no tails, and the odd peasant has lost a toe or two."

"I don't recall ever seeing sheep without ears, or . . ." A nervous laugh escaped her. "It will be all right, Snarls. It's probably just a rumor." Petra glanced over the rest of the groaning, belly-rubbing group and made up her mind. She led them north, to the creek.

At the edge of Hobble-Wobble Creek, with just enough moonlight to cast a shimmer upon the lumps and bumps that bobbed up then disappeared into the water, Petra swallowed hard and wondered at her decision.

"What is that?" Prince Nastybun cowered behind her.

45

"I could fly us over if I felt better," Snarls boasted.

Petra patted Snarls' head, not mentioning the fact that his wings could barely get him off the ground when he didn't have a stomach ache. "Thanks for the offer."

"Look! Those are eyes! It's some kind of monster, isn't it?" Norton screeched.

The puny army moved in to cower behind Norton.

Petra took a deep breath and willed herself to be brave. "I don't think we have monsters here. I don't know what it is, but we're here now, so we'll cross."

"No way," Nastybun protested. The puny army mumbled agreements while pushing and shoving and squeezing until they formed a quivering ball of prince and knights that bumped up against Petra's back.

"We have no choice now." Petra grimaced as she surveyed the mounds in the water. "The forest is too full of those man-eating mosquitoes, and it's too dark to make our way through the trees or to maneuver the bogs. We'll cross here and be on our way in no time."

"I could just blast whatever it is," Snarls offered.

Before Petra could say anything, Snarls took a deep breath and blew out a volcano of smoke and sparks and something that looked like shredded parchment.

"Oops." Snarls faked a grin. "Must be the onions.

They're slightly disagreeing with me."

"Don't worry about it, Snarls. There's no need to blast anything. We'll just walk across calmly and lightly, and before you know it, we'll be on the other side."

Prince Nastybun and his ball of puny knights were now squawking like hungry baby birds in a nest.

Petra had an idea. "In the lands of Pen Pieyu, it is customary to carry an onion for protection," she declared in her strongest knight voice. She handed Norton and each of the tangled knights an onion. "Hang on tight to the onion, do not let it fall. You will be protected.

Snarls let out a little snort laugh. Petra shushed him and raised her onion high above her head.

"Onward soldiers!" she ordered, and led them into the water.

As she waded through the inky black water, wide-eyed and searching, one of the lumps bobbed up in front of her. Two narrow, orange eyes stared at her. Petra stumbled and fell on her butt. The slanted eyes were now eyeball to eyeball with her. Snarls, Norton, and the puny army gasped when Petra reached out to pat the creature's head.

"It's all right, everybody. This is my friend, the

crocodile that frequents the castle moat. I think her name is Letgo, or so I've heard the palace soldiers call her. Oh, and this must be her family," she said when smaller, orange, slanted eyes popped up from beneath the water.

Prince Nastybun and the puny army seemed to roll on the water surface, nearly bowling her over in their race to the other side of the creek. Snarls plucked Petra up by the seat of her pants and skedaddled after them.

After much sighing, groaning, moaning, whimpering, shaking, then cheering, whistling, and teasing, the group proceeded onward to the castle.

At the castle gates, the torch lights were lit, and the orchestra was in full swing blaring out a well-known Baroque melody. Bograt was waiting, leaning on a pillar and tapping her foot. Petra motioned for her to follow along.

Spotting her mother and father on the drawbridge, Petra waved and called out, "I'm home! And I've brought Prince Nastybun and his puny army, and Bograt, the bog witch!"

Petra thought they must look quite the messy sight, for her waving mother stopped waving and flopped over in a faint, and her clapping father stopped clapping and seemed to be stretching up his hair.

The royal councilman fled inside the castle to immediately return with the royal rule book. He tossed the book to land beside the king. The councilman turned and ran.

Meet The Characters Of Book 1

Sir Princess Petra Longstride

Lives at Longstride Castle In Kingdom Pen Pieyu. She is the first and only knight of her kingdom.

Birthday: September 9.

Age: 9 year.

Middle name: Brettania (middle name after her grandmother, Brettania May Longstride, the great story teller).

Favorite color: pink.

Favorite foods: chocolate, mushrooms, olives, nuts, wild berries.

Favorite activities: archery, jousting, Highland dancing, storytelling, riding her steed, javelin tossing, home-school lessons, onion throwing, polishing her armour, making mud pies, and her most favorite activity, adventures.

Dislikes: big meanies, eating anything with onions in it, big birds, bees.

Parent's names: King William Kuff Longstride and Queen Mabel Viola Longstride.

Snarls the Dragon
Lives nearby and inside and around Dragon Mountain in The Forest of Doom.
Birthday: October 23.
Age: 3 (that equals 12 in people years).
Middle name: Lotzapuf (middle name after his mother's father, Singe Burnett Lotzapuf).
Last name: Doom. Hence, why the Forest of Doom is called the Forest of Doom.
Favorite color: shiny silver things.
Favorite foods: onions, hors d'oeuvres with onions.
Favorite activities: cooking, barbeques, parties, adventures.
Dislikes: falling rocks, being chased, fear of losing his tail, explosions, indigestion.

Bograt the Bog Witch
Lives in the bogs and swamps smack-in-the middle of all the other lands of all the other kingdoms, and just at the edge of Hobble-Wobble Creek.
Birthday: February 30 (that's what her birth certificate says).
Age: she counts 10 years by the succession of seasons.
Real name: Marsheesh Mya Mire.
Favorite color: black.
Favorite foods: onions, broccoli, carrots, lettuce, squash--pretty much anything that is a vegetable, and nuts.
Favorite activities: chasing frogs, scaring people (well, only a little), cooking with onions, eating onion anything, picking mushrooms, mud baths, making deals, exploring.
Dislikes: frilly dresses, frilly dresses with lace, dresses, water baths.

Prince Nastybun
Lives in the very wet and soggy lands of Kingdom
Mesoggie, just east and a little north of the Kingdom of
Crablips.
Birthday: June 1.
Age: 10 years.
First name: Norton.
Middle name: Hiney (This was very hard information
to come by, and nobody, until now, knew of his middle
name).
Favorite color: purple.
Favorite foods: asparagus, mushrooms, squid
(although he rarely gets to eat squid because squid
comes from the West Sea, and he lives far away from
the West Sea).
Favorite activities: riding his pony, commanding his
puny army, spear throwing, drying off, parties,
exploring.
Dislikes: dancing, falling off his pony, soggy boots,
moss on his armour, monsters and other scary things.

King and Queen Longstride
Rulers, owners, and directors of Kingdom Pen Pieyu where they maintain, direct, pay the castle bills, and rule Longstride Castle and the surrounding lands of Pen Pieyu. Also, Petra's parents.
King's name, birthday, age: King William Kuff Longstride, January 1, 52 years of age.
Queen's name, birthday, age: Queen Mabel Viola Longstride, January 3, 41 years of age.
King's favorite foods: octopus stew, octopus crepes, fancy finger foods, cake.
King's favorite activities: being the lord and boss of his kingdom.
Queen's favorite foods: coconut shrimp, coconut cream pie, coconut milk.
Queen's favorite activities: practicing a faint that doesn't mess her hairdo, polishing her jewelry, ruling her husband's kingdom.
King's dislikes: women trying to rule his kingdom.
Queen's dislikes: kings who think women can't rule a kingdom.

Synopsis of Sir Princess Petra's Talent Book 2

King Longstride has written a new rule in the royal rule book that declares all Princess Knights of Kingdom Pen Pieyu (Petra is still the only knight in the lands of Pen Pieyu) must attend Talent School and acquire a princess talent certificate or suffer the consequences of the royal magician's spell to be turned into a frog to live in the bogs for five years.

Of course, the king writes these rules to deter Petra from her silly knight nonsense and act more like a princess. And of course, Petra wants no part of being a girly princess.

But when Petra believes that the royal magician has turned all nine of the palace soldiers into frogs she, reluctantly, agrees to go.

Petra and Snarls (the dragon who is now her royal steed and co-adventurer, and also the head chef at Longstride Castle) head off for the Land of Lost Donkeys, where King Asterman awaits her arrival at Talent School.

En route to Talent School, the adventurers meet a very strange knight named Prince Duce Crablips from the

Kingdom of Crablips who declares a duel with Petra.

Okay, so the dueling thing was all over a silly misunderstanding, but once they straighten that all out (and only one small injury is sustained by Snarls), Petra and Duce become friends and the trio all head off to Talent School.

Snarls joins Barbeque School. Duce decides on Crochet School. And Petra is left to choose amongst some very undesirable schools: Princess Etiquette School, Knitting School, Cloak Sewing School, Get Over Fainting Fast School, Jewelry Budgeting School, Preparing to Be Engaged School. There is, however, one quite intriguing school that, due to a technical error on King Asterman's part, does not have the proper *Closed* sign posted.

Well, Petra does choose a Talent School, and she does a pretty good job of it by using her very good imagination and, hence, attaining a talent certificate. But her new talent is not quite what the king had in mind for his princess daughter.

After Snarls pulls a somewhat klutzy manoeuvre in Barbeque School, the trio has to skedaddle—Talent School is definitely over.

On their way back to Kingdom Pen Pieyu, Petra spots

a dilapidated sign on a tree—a sign with warnings posted by the ganutes of the Vast Wilderness (a land where no adventurer has ventured before). Petra decides they should explore.

The ganutes have an attack first questions later strategy. Once this chaos is all sorted out, somehow, this all leads to someone else becoming a knight.

Back at Longstride Castle, Petra announces her new talent, introduces a bunch of ganutes for potential knights, and declares the newest knight of Pen Pieyu—all of this being a very big shock to the king and queen.

But Petra has a way of smoothing things over. She shares her new talent with the kingdom at the newest knight's knighting party.

All is well in the Kingdom of Pen Pieyu. And Pen Pieyu Kingdom will never, ever be the same.

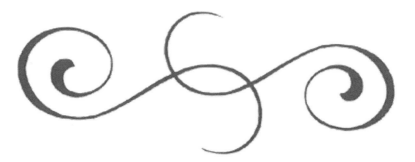

Meet The New Characters Of Book 2

Prince Duce Crablips
Lives in the Kingdom of Crablips, just west and a little south of the Kingdom of Mesoggie.
Birthday: July 8.
Age: 10 years.
Middle name: Anise (after the aromatic herb that was in bloom at his birth).
Favorite color: pinkish hues, pink-like shades, pink tones, pink.
Favorite foods: hors d'oeuvres and dainty pastries.
Favorite activities: crocheting, needlework, being told stories, sing-song get-togethers.
Dislikes: shadows, dark places, fires, things being thrown at him—especially in the dark.

The Royal Magician
Lives at Pen Pieyu Castle, in a secret room, at the very top of the invisible tower.
Name: Lentil Leigh Keynus.
Birthday: May 10.
Age: 111 years.
Favorite color: sparkles.
Favorite foods: frog soup, eye-of-toad rolled in fish skins, spider leg cookies.
Favorite activities: trying out secret spells in the castle tower's secret closet.
Dislikes: small closets, fake magicians.

King Asterman

Lives in the Kingdom of Lost Donkeys, north of the Kingdom of Pen Pieyu, and is the headmaster of Talent School.

Full name: Adler Ameba Asterman.

Birthday: April 21.

Age: 71 years.

Favorite color: red.

Favorite foods: cherry pie, tomato soup, steamed radishes, rosehip jelly.

Favorite activities: reading, writing, teaching, inventing new classes for Talent School, sometimes looking for the lost donkeys.

Dislikes: know-it-alls, fire episodes, explosions, always looking for the lost donkeys.

Synopsis of Sir Princess Petra's Mission
Book 3

King Longstride has, again, written a new rule in the royal rule book to try and deter Sir Princess Petra from her knightly ways. This new rule, a mission, requires Petra, along with her faithful dragon steed, Snarls, to venture into the Kingdom of Boogy Gobees to capture a vicious, notorious-fabled, and possibly dragon-eating car-panther and bring it back to Kingdom Pen Pieyu or forfeit her knighthood once and for all.

Petra, Snarls, and Bograt (Bograt has no choice but to go, it's part of this new rule in the royal rule book) start off together on their journey to find a vicious, notorious-fabled car-panther—until they lose Bograt, who is swept away by a wave.

This leaves only Petra and Snarls to figure out what a car-panther is, how dangerous the creature really is, where to find the creature once they reach Kingdom Boogy Gobees, and just how they will manage to capture a car-panther.

Of course, no adventure proceeds without obstacles in the way, so when Snarls suddenly disappears, Petra is left on her own to figure things out.

After some commotion, chaos, and ruckus, Petra, Snarls, and Bograt are reunited just as they meet their first car-panther. Yikes!

The car-panther leads the Pen Pieyu trio off to Hobnobby Castle in Kingdom Boogy Gobees where the trio find out not all is as it seems. Petra, Snarls, and Bograt to an extent, join forces, not to capture a car-panther but to help the car-panthers save Hobnobby Castle.

After King Hobnobby grants a couple of knighthoods, and one knighthood is refused by a potential knight, the trio head home to face the consequences of Petra's lost knighthood of Kingdom Pen Pieyu since she has failed her mission by not returning with a vicious, notorious-fabled car-panther.

Due to a technicality in the royal rule book, the situation takes a sudden turn when it is recognized that Kingdom Pen Pieyu now has three royal knights (instead of none) to its honor. And, for sure and absolutely, Pen Pieyu Kingdom will never be the same.

Meet The New Characters Of Book 3

Findor Woodrow
Lives in the Kingdom of Boogy Gobees, east of Kingdom Pen Pieyu. Findor is Elvish and the head workman in the Elvish kingdom.
Full name: Findor Redwood Woodrow.
Birthday: July 8.
Age: 54 elvish years (about 14 people years).
Favorite color: brown.
Favorite foods: moss stew, mushroom soup, berry pie, anise tea.
Favorite activities: joking around, sculpting, inventing.

Dislikes: things that fall down, people who hurt trees.

King Hobnobby
Lives in Kingdom Boogy Gobees at Hobnobby Castle and is the Elvish king.
Full name: Theodor Thomas Henry Hobnobby.
Birthday: Dec. 11.
Age: 217 elvish years (approximately 54 people years).
Favorite color: yellow.
Favorite foods: moss stew, beat soup, lentil bread, tiger lily tea.
Favorite activities: being king.
Dislikes: lumpy, bumpy things, people who cut down trees.

Character Sketches
by the
Author

Sir Princess Petra

Snarls

Bograt The Bog Witch

Prince Norton Nastybun

Prince Duce Crablips

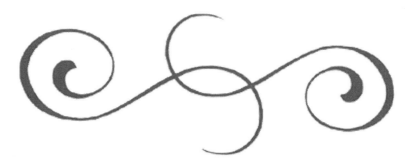

If you enjoyed reading Sir Princess Petra, reviews are always appreciated by the author. Reviews can be posted on:

Amazon
Barnes & Noble
Goodreads

Sign up for The Dragon Newsletter to receive your free 55-page Sir Princess Petra coloring book:

https://dragonsbook.com/subscribe/

Author website: https://www.dragonsbook.com

Made in the USA
Columbia, SC
21 November 2020

25145941R00061